Mia and Molly are twins.
They look the same
and they like the same things.
But they are also different in many ways!

A lovely flip book about similarities
and differences—and twins!
For toddlers ages 24 months and up,
with a focus on the child's daily life.

Mia and Molly
The Same

Mylo Freeman

Clavis
NEW YORK

Look—**Mia and Molly** are twins.
They look the same.

Today **Mia and Molly** are wearing the same clothes and the same shoes.

They both love the same pink bunny
and like to sit on the same red chairs.

And at night **Mia and Molly** go to sleep in beds that look exactly the same.

Mia and Molly both use a pink potty.

They both love chocolate ice cream.

But sometimes **Mia and Molly** find it hard to share the same cuddly frog . . .

It is a good thing that Mommy has a big hug for both of them to share!

When it's time for bed,

Mia and Molly both want
a cuddle with Daddy.

Sleep well, **Mia and Molly**!

Mia is sleepy after bath time,
but **Molly** is not.
Molly wants to keep playing
with her rubber duck.

When they take their bath,
Mia washes her toy fish and
Molly splashes with a little rubber duck.

Mia and Molly both like
to walk in the rain.
Molly wears her pink boots;
Mia wears green.

Mia loves to laugh at silly puppets.

Molly thinks they are a little bit scary.

Mia likes to dress up
in her frog suit.
Molly would rather dress up
as a bunny.

Molly loves eating tomatoes.

And **Mia**? She would like nothing better than to eat bananas every day.

Look—**Mia and Molly** are twins.
They look the same,
but they like different things.
Mia loves reading books,
and Molly likes to play with her ball.

Mia and Molly
Different

Mylo Freeman

Clavis

NEW YORK